Constance C. Greene

ODDS ON OLIVER

Illustrations by S. D. Schindler

VIKING

This book is for
OLIVER GREENE RADWAN,
on whom I'll place odds
any day in the week

VIKING
Published by the Penguin Group
Penguin Books USA Inc., 375 Hudson Street, New York, New York 10014, U.S.A.
Penguin Books Ltd, 27 Wrights Lane, London W8 5TZ, England
Penguin Books Australia Ltd, Ringwood, Victoria, Australia
Penguin Books Canada Ltd, 10 Alcorn Avenue,
Toronto, Ontario, Canada M4V 3B2
Penguin Books (N.Z.) Ltd, 182–190 Wairau Road, Auckland 10, New Zealand
Penguin Books Ltd, Registered Offices: Harmondsworth, Middlesex, England

First published in 1993 by Viking, a division of Penguin Books USA Inc.

1   3   5   7   9   10   8   6   4   2

Text copyright © Constance C. Greene, 1993
Illustrations copyright © S.D. Schindler, 1993
All rights reserved

Library of Congress Cataloging-in-Publication Data
Greene, Constance C. Odds on Oliver / by Constance C. Greene :
illustrated by S.D. Schindler.   p.   cm.
Summary: Oliver's attempts to be a hero result in such humorous
disasters as going up a tree to rescue a cat and getting stuck himself.
ISBN 0-670-84549-3
[1. Heroes—Fiction.   2. Humorous stories.]
I. Schindler, S.D., ill.   II. Title.
PZ7.G82870d   1993   [Fic]—dc20   92-25932   CIP   AC

Printed in U.S.A.   Set in 13 point Primer
Without limiting the rights under copyright reserved above, no part of this
publication may be reproduced, stored in or introduced into a retrieval system,
or transmitted, in any form or by any means (electronic, mechanical,
photocopying, recording or otherwise), without the prior written permission
of both the copyright owner and the above publisher of this book.

CONTENTS

☆ 1 ☆
CARROT HILL

"All right, boys and girls." Ms. Mabel, the head of Carrot Hill Nursery School, clapped her hands. "Anyone who has to use the bathroom, hold up two fingers, please."

"How will that help?" Oliver said.

Arthur laughed. Oliver held up two fingers and waved them around. Then he bopped Arthur on the head to show he wanted to be friends.

Everyone giggled.

"We are here to learn, class," Ms. Mabel said. "To write our names and to be responsible people. To go down the slide and to draw." She paused and looked around the room. "A show of hands, please. How many of you have a pet?"

Arthur held up his hand and said, "I have a pet fish. She sleeps in her tank and sometimes she lets me pet her."

Oliver held up his hand.

"All right, Oliver," Ms. Mabel said patiently. "Tell us about your pet."

"I have a dog and her name is Edna. Her hair is the same color as mine," Oliver said. "When I'm five, I'm going to be a hero."

The class rustled like leaves in the fall. Somebody burped.

Oliver burped back.

"Yes, well, Edna is a lovely name," Ms. Mabel said. "My mother's name was Edna."

Oliver bopped Arthur on the head again.

"Order, please, boys and girls." Ms. Mabel frowned. "We are here to learn to shake hands and to look the person we're shaking hands with straight in the eye."

"Boys don't shake hands," Oliver said.

"That's what you think," Ms. Mabel said.

A girl with pigtails held up her hand. "I have a pet pig named Pig," the girl said. Oliver pulled one of her pigtails and the girl bopped Oliver on the head to get even.

That was pretty much how the first day at Carrot Hill Nursery School went.

After that things went downhill fast. One wet and windy Wednesday, Ms. Mabel reached the end of her rope. She had had it. Plus, she had a terrible head cold and felt something awful.

When Oliver and Arthur started in with the bops again, Ms. Mabel knew what she had to do.

"I hab ward you ab ward you to stop the bopping," Ms. Mabel said. "Wod of you bust go. We bust hab order in Carrot Hill. We will draw straws. The wod who gets the short straw bust go."

Oliver got the short straw.

"Oliver bust go," said Ms. Mabel sadly, for she liked all the boys and girls at Carrot Hill.

"Go where?" Oliver said.

"Oud." Ms. Mabel pointed to the door.

"But I just got here," Oliver said. Nevertheless he packed his backpack and never looked back.

"Where did I go wrong?" Oliver's mother cried. "He's only four and already he's a dropout. What's to become of him? Poor little Oliver."

"Poor little Oliver my foot," said Oliver's dad. "He's no dropout, he's a kickout. Give the kid a break. He's young, he'll learn. I'll lay odds on Oliver any day in the week."

"But he was in the top ten percentile!" Oliver's mother cried. "Brainwise, that is. Which would look very, very good on his resumé."

"What does *odds* mean?" Oliver asked.

"It means I'll put my money on you anytime, Ol," said his dad. "It means you're a winner in my estimation."

Oliver listened carefully. Two words caught his attention. One was *money* and the other was *winner*.

His mouth stretched as wide as any Halloween pumpkin's and his spiky orange hair fairly crackled and his freckles seemed to march across his nose like a trail of ants in search of the sugar bowl.

"Odds on me!" Oliver shouted, full of joy. "Odds on me!"

☆ 2 ☆

THE BLUE BURD

Oliver's mom and dad ran the Blue Burd restaurant down on North Main Street. When the sign painter goofed and spelled *bird* B-U-R-D Oliver's dad had jumped up and down in frustration and pulled so hard on his mustache that it brought tears to his eyes.

Then the *Daily Blab* had run a picture of the sign on its front page. That got a good laugh. Customers started to pour in.

The ring of the cash register was deafening.

Oliver's mom and dad decided to leave the sign be. "Blue Burd" had a nice ring to it, they decided, just like the cash register. They even had cards printed up.

BLUE BURD RESTAURANT, the cards said. GIVE YOURSELF A TREAT! MAKE YOURSELF HAPPY! THE BLUE BURD IS THE BURD OF HAPPINESS!

Oliver's dad made the Tex-Mex chili. It was so hot that the entire fire department always came for a bowlful on their night off. Oliver's dad also baked the pies. The coconut cream and lemon meringue were especially outstanding.

Oliver's mom ran the cleanup detail, on account of she'd been in the army. You could eat off her floors.

"You could eat off my floors," she'd say proudly.

And, on a certain hot night in June, the day after Oliver skidded out of fourth grade, headlong on his way toward fifth, that's exactly what they did.

This particular evening, the Blue Burd was jumping and Oliver was helping out.

He felt lucky, as if this might be the night he'd be a hero. He poured out ice water and brought the glasses round to the tables. Folks drank gallons of ice water to douse the fire the Tex-Mex chili set in their throats.

Just when it seemed that the evening had reached its peak and that things couldn't possibly get any more exciting, the door to the Blue Burd burst open and in came U. Crumm, Town Clerk.

A hush fell. You could have heard a pin drop. And why this awed silence? U. Crumm was a big shot. She didn't eat just anywhere. When she put her O.K. on a place, that place became famous overnight.

Oliver's dad took off his tall white chef's hat and wiped his hands on it. He shook hands all round, even with Oliver.

"Pleased to meet you," Oliver's dad said to U. Crumm. "This is my wife and this is my boy, Oliver. We're one big happy family here. Unfortunately, we're all full up at the moment. It'll be a short wait. In the meantime, try one of my world-famous chocolate-chip cookies."

Well, U. Crumm was a class-A eater. In her youth, she had won every single eating contest in the state. And a few outside of it. Chicken, watermelon, pancakes, you name it. U. Crumm was a champion when it came to putting away the groceries.

Bar none.

The short wait turned into a long one. No one, it seemed, wanted to leave the Blue Burd. They were having too good a time. They all had seconds on the Tex-Mex chili and thirds on the pies. Finally, noticing that U. Crumm was getting restless, not to mention she'd inhaled every chocolate-chip cookie in the place, Oliver's dad suggested she eat on the shining, spotless floor.

"Fine and dandy," said U. Crumm. "I'm not proud. What's good enough for the common people is good enough for me."

Oliver's dad brought the knives and forks and napkins and Oliver rushed back for more ice water and salt and pepper and U. Crumm plopped down, all set for a feast.

That night U. Crumm outdid herself. She had six helpings of Tex-Mex chili and seven of pie. Oliver kept count.

When U. Crumm went to get up, she couldn't. It took Oliver's dad and three other men to hoist her to her feet. Plus Oliver, who got under U. Crumm and pushed.

Just as she was getting her sea legs and had teetered to a standing position, U. Crumm slipped on a stray piece of ice from her water glass and crash-landed smack on Oliver.

Oliver let out a squeak and blacked out.

A long sigh went up. This was turning out to be the most exciting evening most folks had had in ages. They stopped eating and waited to see what would happen next.

The chief of police, who had snuck away from his desk for some chili, snapped, "Everybody freeze!"

Nobody paid any attention, as usual.

When Oliver came to, he could barely breathe, smushed as he was underneath U. Crumm. He heard Arthur, who had come to chow down at the Blue Burd with his

11

mom and dad because it was his mom's bowling night and she liked to rest her arm, shout, "She hit him like a ton of bricks! He'll never get out of there alive!"

U. Crumm blushed a bright red color. She didn't like lying there with all the wind knocked out of her and her skirt hiked up so that everyone in the restaurant could see the big hole in the knee of her panty hose.

Finally, with a good deal of pushing and shoving and grunting and groaning, Oliver's dad and several burly firefighters tied one end of a thick rope around U. Crumm's middle and swung the other end over a rafter. Then they lifted her off Oliver and into midair. For a few moments, she spun there like a top. Then they lowered the rope and U. Crumm set foot on solid ground once more.

Oliver lay there feeling as flat as any possum run over by a tractor-trailer. He was sure his arms and legs looked as if they'd been ironed. He did *not* look like a hero, he thought sadly.

"My baby, my baby!" Oliver's mom cried in a loud voice. Oliver was so embarrassed, he felt like going through the floor. On the other hand, he'd just been saved from doing exactly that. So he jumped to his feet to prove he was as good as new.

"Hip hip hooray!" the customers shouted in unison.

"Odds on Oliver!" Oliver's dad cried.

Oliver's mom frowned and said, "Are those your good pants?"

"Whew!" said Arthur, wiping his brow in an exaggerated way. "I thought you were a goner."

"Don't you wish," said Oliver.

Next morning, a package came to Oliver's house by special delivery. Inside was a super-deluxe fishing rod, the most expensive kind.

Just what Oliver had wanted for ages.

The card said, *Thanks for a lovely evening.*

It was signed *U. Crumm, Town Clerk.*

☆ 3 ☆
GONE FISHING

Oliver and Arthur dropped everything and went fishing. Edna went too. Edna liked to bark at the fish. Sometimes the fish barked back. Those were the dogfish.

"I can't miss with this," Oliver said, waving his new rod. "Hand me a marshmallow, Arthur."

"We ate all the marshmallows," Arthur said. "All we got left is worms."

"Marshmallows are better bait," Oliver said.

"This bozo smells," Arthur said, handing over a worm.

"You'd smell too if you'd croaked as long ago as he did," Oliver said.

The mosquitoes dive-bombed them, the sun walked across the sky, and the fish were not biting.

"This is getting very boring," Arthur said.

In the distance, Edna barked. Long and loud.

"Probably she's going for a jackrabbit," Oliver said. "She likes to chase jackrabbits even if she never catches one."

"Sort of like you and fishing," Arthur said.

"Whoa!" Oliver hollered. He had a bite. "Hang on! It's a whopper! It's a monster goon shark. I can see his razor-sharp teeth and his mean yellow eyes."

"Sounds like a tiger shark to me," Arthur said. "I read a book about tiger sharks. They eat people."

"Get the net!" Oliver shouted.

"Where is it?" Arthur said.

"I don't know! He's getting away! Get the net, Arthur!"

"It's not here," Arthur said. "Somebody must have stolen it."

"Come hold the line!" Oliver yelled. "I'll find it."

By the time Oliver found the net under a nearby willow tree and raced back, Arthur was floundering in the water.

"Help! Help!" Arthur cried.

Arthur didn't like to get his face wet. He hated to put his face underwater, so he'd only learned how to dog-paddle.

"Are you drowning, Arthur?" Oliver called. He shucked off his black hightops, which luckily were untied, and stripped down to his black-and-white polka-dot boxer shorts. Then he plunged in to rescue his friend. He did a fast crawl toward Arthur.

"Glub, glub," Arthur said. He did *not* sound good.

"Hang on!" Oliver cried. "I'm coming!"

Just as Oliver reached Arthur, Arthur stood up and said, "Chill out, dude, I can touch bottom. It's not as deep as I thought."

"Where's the shark?" Oliver said.

"He got away."

"That's the last time I try to rescue *you*," Oliver said disgustedly, heading for shore. "Next time you can just sink. See if I care."

"Can I help it if I didn't drown?" Arthur said.

Edna watched, grinning.

"What's so funny?" Oliver said to her.

Edna's mouth turned up at the corners even more. Oliver thought he heard her say *ha ha* but he couldn't be sure.

"Go soak your head," Oliver said to both of them.

"I already did," said Arthur.

☆ 4 ☆

STICKUP

The next day, Oliver's mom sent him to the store to buy a half-gallon of fat-free milk. When he took the milk to the express checkout, a woman in front of him was already unloading her cart.

"It says ten items only," Oliver said, pointing to the sign. "She's got about fifty-two items."

The checkout girl and the woman in front of him acted as if they hadn't heard. As her groceries were rung up, the woman packed them herself, and speedily too, putting the eggs on top so they wouldn't break. Oliver figured she'd probably been a checkout girl herself once and knew the ropes.

"There you go, Aunt Lucy," the checkout girl said, glaring at Oliver. Aunt Lucy handed over some money and wheeled her laden cart away at a fast trot.

A man behind Oliver said in a loud voice, "The world's full of chiselers, sonny."

"You want plastic or paper?" the girl said, ringing up the milk.

The man stumbled and lurched against Oliver. It was his first stickup and he wasn't too good a stickup man.

"I don't need a bag," Oliver said. "I'll take it like it is."

"This here is a stickup," the man said. "Don't nobody move."

Oliver pocketed the change.

"I got a gun," the man said.

A long arm swooped around and circled Oliver's neck.

Oliver was so surprised, he didn't struggle or cry out.

The man thrust a battered canvas bag

across the counter and said, "Fill 'er up, girlie," like a person at a gas station. "And don't bother me with the small stuff. I want tens and twenties. I got no time for ones."

"You're choking me," Oliver managed to say.

"One false move and the kid gets it," the man said.

The checkout girl gave a little squawk, like a scared chicken.

"*Awkk,*" she said.

"Don't give me no lip," the man said. "I got a gun, don't forget."

Oliver wondered if it might somehow be April Fools' Day, even though as far as he knew it was still June. The light coming in the store window was blinding, so bright it was giving him a headache. He saw a mail truck drive by outside, heard loud teenage music blaring. The man's jacket smelled of rotting fruit. Bananas, mostly.

Oliver opened his mouth to shout "Help!" but nothing came out.

21

"I'm closed for the day," the girl said, putting out her CLOSED sign.

"Don't give me any of that," the man said. "I've had a tough day."

You've had a tough day, Oliver thought.

"The cash, girlie, the cash," the man said.

The girl fumbled with the cash drawer.

"It's stuck," she said.

The man's arm tightened around Oliver's neck. "Get it open fast, or else I might have to blow the kid's brains out," he said.

Oliver considered throwing up. It is a well-known fact that people don't like to hang on to a person who is throwing up.

"It's jammed." The girl poked at the drawer. "Maybe if you . . ."

The man loosened his grip on Oliver and leaned over the counter to give the cash register a few pokes. It stayed closed.

"Here's where it's sticking," the girl said. "Try again."

The man leaned even closer to get a good

look, and the checkout girl grabbed his arm and twisted it behind him. Oliver thought he heard something snap. The man howled and let go of Oliver completely.

"Register five!" the checkout girl hollered. "Attempted robbery!"

"*Ooowww!*" the man howled.

A sudden flurry of activity took place. The store manager and the butcher came running. The butcher wore a dirty white apron and the store manager wore a very nervous expression.

"Good work, Lila," the manager said when the butcher had subdued the robber and led him away. Oliver wondered if the butcher was going to lock the robber in the meat freezer until the cops came.

"Fast thinking," the manager went on. "I'll see you get a commendation from the top brass for this."

"I'd rather have a week off with pay," said Lila.

"How'd you do it?" asked the manager.

"I got my brown belt in karate last week," Lila said.

The manager noticed Oliver for the first time. "Here, son," he said, scooping up a handful of Milky Ways and Snickers bars from the display shelf. He stuffed them into Oliver's hands.

"He was gonna blow the kid's brains out," Lila remarked.

When Oliver got home his mother asked, "Where's the milk?"

"I musta left it on the counter," Oliver said.

"Good thing your head is fastened on tight or you'd forget that too," Oliver's mom said.

Oliver went into the bathroom and locked the door. He blew on the mirror and wrote his name in the foggy circle his breath made.

Oliver was here, he wrote. You blew it, he thought sadly. You blew it.

At *this* rate he'd never make hero, he realized.

He unlocked the bathroom door and went back to the kitchen.

His mom was on the telephone. When

she hung up, he said, "Mom, can I take karate lessons?"

"We'll see," his mother said.

Which probably meant no, Oliver thought glumly.

☆ 5 ☆

UP A TREE

"The guy was really weird," Oliver said. "So he gets me by my neck and he goes like this . . ." Oliver demonstrated, using Arthur's neck.

"Quit it," Arthur said. "That hurts."

"Then the checkout girl twists his arm and I think she broke it," Oliver went on. "I even heard it snap. She's got this brown belt in karate. She was a hero. The guy was going to blow my brains out."

"Maybe you could sell this to the movies," Arthur said. "Then they'd make it into a sitcom and you'd be rich and famous."

"A stretch limo with two gold telephones wouldn't be bad," Oliver said dreamily.

"Listen, Ol, I wrote a short story," Arthur said. "Beany Allen says Ms. Carbery makes you write a short story in fifth grade, so I'm getting a head start. Listen."

"Hold it," Oliver said. "I'm tired. I almost got my brains blown out today. I don't want to hear your dumb short story."

Arthur pulled a piece of paper and a pen from his pocket. Then he cleared his throat and read: " 'It was a dark and stormy night.' "

"You stole that from Snoopy," Oliver said. "Snoopy always starts his stories like that."

"So? Snoopy's only a dog," Arthur said.

"Better not let Edna hear you say that," Oliver said. "She'd take your arm off."

"I need help, Ol. I'm stuck. I got writer's block," Arthur said. "Think of something to go after 'night.' "

Oliver thought. "How about 'The space ship burst open and a tribe of monster mutant aliens oozing purple slime came out.' "

"Excellent, excellent," Arthur said, writing furiously. "Keep going, Ol."

"Well, the tribe of aliens decides to set fire to the school," Oliver said slowly.

"Neato," said Arthur.

"So they set fire to the school by rubbing their fingernails together," Oliver went on. "Get it? Instead of rubbing two sticks together or using matches, they rub their fingernails together on account of their fingernails are like matches."

"I read in a book that if you bite your fingernails and swallow them," Arthur said, "a hand will grow inside your stomach."

"Try it," Oliver said.

"What do I want a hand inside my stomach for?" Arthur replied.

"So when the doc opens you up to take out your appendix, he freaks. He sees that ol' hand sitting there and he runs screaming out of the hospital and he's never seen or heard from again," Oliver said.

"My appendix is already out," Arthur said.

"Oliver!" Oliver's mom called. "Mrs. Murphy's on the phone. She says Edna chased Charlie up a tree again. Better get over there and get Charlie down before Mr. Murphy gets home."

Mr. Murphy got sore when Edna chased Charlie up a tree. Besides, it was the third time this week.

"Creepola Charlie," Oliver grumbled. "Why can't that cat get down on his own? He got up, he can get down."

"Edna's definitely out of line," Arthur said. "She has no business chasing Charlie up a tree."

"That's what dogs are supposed to do, chase cats up trees," Oliver said. "It's the law of nature."

Oliver went to the kichen, grabbed a can of tuna fish from the cupboard, and walked to the Murphys' house. Arthur split. He hated the smell of tuna fish.

"Oh, Oliver, I'm glad to see you!" said Mrs. Murphy. "Do something! Mr. Murphy said once more and he's had it! Not to mention Edna."

Oliver put the tuna fish can under the tree. "This oughta do it," he said.

They waited. No Charlie. Edna lay down and put her head between her paws, pretending she was thinking.

"Guess I'll have to go up and bring him down," said Oliver, puffing out his chest. This was his big chance, he thought excitedly. Today was hero day.

"Oh, Oliver, can you?" Mrs. Murphy said. "He's way up at the top. I don't want you to hurt yourself."

"Piece of cake," Oliver said heroically. He went up the tree like a pro, swinging from branch to branch, yodeling like Tarzan calling the apes.

The tree seemed to grow even as Oliver climbed. This was some tall tree, all right.

There was Charlie, licking his leg, taking things easy.

"Hey, creepola," Oliver said, and he stretched out a hand to grab Charlie. Charlie hissed and raked an open claw across Oliver's hand, drawing blood.

"Yow!" Oliver yelled.

Charlie streaked past, on his way down, under his own steam. Brave as a lion, Charlie was.

The branch Oliver was standing on gave way. Oliver grabbed another branch with his good hand and hung in space, swinging in the wind, sucking his own blood.

"Oliver!" Mrs. Murphy's voice sounded very far away. "Are you all right?"

"No!" Oliver yelled back. He knew he'd blown it one more time.

Oliver hung on and felt around with his feet for another branch to light on.

Don't look down, he told himself. The worst thing you can do is to look down.

He looked down. Instantly he became dizzy. A crowd had gathered down below. He heard the wail of a siren.

I could go for a free fall, Oliver thought. Like a parachuter. He had always admired the jaunty way parachuters stepped out of the airplane, as calmly as if they were going to the corner store for a newspaper. Or a half-gallon of fat-free milk.

If only he had a parachute.

His feet kept going, kicking back and forth, looking for something to land on. Maybe he'd try for a free fall anyway.

"Hang on! We're on our way!" a voice called.

Better make it snappy, Oliver thought as he felt his good hand slipping fast.

"Gotcha!" the fireman said as Oliver fell, like a ripe peach, right into the man's hands.

Down on the ground, Mrs. Murphy kissed Oliver, and bought four tickets to the Firemen's Ball. Charlie was nowhere to be seen. Edna hid behind a tree.

"All right for you, Edna." Oliver spoke sternly to Edna's tail. "Next time you can get that danged cat down yourself. If you fall out of the tree, see if I care."

Edna wagged her tail sheepishly, and Oliver patted her head. "You're a cool cat, Edna," he said, "even if you are a dog."

☆ 6 ☆

HAVAHART

The Blue Burd was gearing up for a gala
Fourth of July party. Everyone in town was
invited.

"Fill up these garbage bags, boys," Oliver's dad said to Oliver and Arthur. "Let's
make the place shine. Start in the shed.
There's stuff there that's almost as old as
the Declaration of Independence."

Oliver's dad placed his hand over his
heart as he recited: " 'We hold these truths
to be self-evident, that all men are created
equal.' "

"That's the Declaration of Independence," Oliver said. "My dad knows it by heart."

"I know what it is," Arthur said. "Think I'm a dummy?"

They went to the shed and the first thing Oliver saw was his old Havahart trap.

"Hey, look, my Havahart trap!" Oliver cried. "So this is where it was. I've been looking for it for a long time. Now we can catch a woodchuck. Maybe a muskrat too."

"What do we do with it after we catch it?" Arthur said.

"Let it go," Oliver said. "Back to its native habitat. After we study it up close."

Oliver found other good stuff. Beat-up hubcaps, a stack of ancient license plates going as far back as 1962, a battered felt hat with a wide brim.

"That's my dad's gangster hat," Oliver said.

Arthur's eyes opened wide. "Your dad was a gangster?"

"Nah, he wore it to high school," Oliver said. "With a vest and all."

"Weird," Arthur said. "Really, really weird."

After they loaded the bulging garbage bags filled with junk into the back of Oliver's dad's truck, Oliver's dad gave them each a dollar. "For a job well done," he said.

At dusk, Oliver and Arthur lugged the Havahart trap into the woods behind Oliver's house. The woods were black and full of night noises—spooky, creaking sounds that made shivers run up and down their spines and raised the hair on the backs of their necks.

"Oho-oho-ohooo," something sang in the night.

"Wha-wha-what's that?" Arthur stammered, following Oliver so closely that he kept stepping on Oliver's heels.

"Might be an owl," Oliver said, faking calm. "Might be a ghost."

Arthur rejected the idea of ghosts hands-down. "Beany Allen said he heard there were woodchucks as big as bears around here," he said loudly, toughing it out.

A branch snapped. The wind rose and a lone bat sailed across the sky.

"Beany Allen is full of it," Oliver said.

Oliver dropped into the trap the contents of one of the Blue Burd doggy bags he'd brought along for bait.

"Listen!" Arthur grabbed Oliver's arm. "I hear it! It's coming to get us. Let's go, Ol!"

Oliver hit the dirt and lay flat, like an infantryman. If only I'd worn my camouflage suit, he thought, I'd be invisible.

"I don't hear anything," he said.

"It sounds like a monster," Arthur said as the crashing sound came closer.

"We could dig a hole and hide," Oliver said. He could hear a heart beating and didn't know if it was his or Arthur's.

A shape hurtled out at them from the darkness.

"*Aarrrgghhh!*" Arthur cried.

"No!" Oliver shouted. "No, you're not getting us!"

He felt something wet against his face.

Something wet and rough, like a dog's tongue.

"It's only Edna!" Oliver yelled. "Edna, for Pete's sake!"

"I knew it all along," Arthur said. He got up and brushed himself off. "Give Edna a treat, Ol," he said. "Give her the other doggy bag, why doncha?"

"Nah," Oliver said. "Edna hates left-overs."

☆ 7 ☆

SKUNKED

The next morning, the trap was empty, the food from the doggy bag gone.

Oliver dropped to his hands and knees and sniffed the ground.

"Bear tracks, most likely," he said.

"Looks like cougar droppings to me," Arthur said.

When they got back to the Blue Burd, the restaurant was humming. Extra help skimmed around, chopping, peeling, shredding, whistling.

"Heap big blast," Arthur said. He had just read a book about Indians and apparently that was the way they talked.

"Who's setting off the fireworks, Dad?" Oliver said.

"U. Crumm," his dad replied.

"Better nail down the refreshments, then," Oliver said. "U. Crumm's a class-A eater, don't forget."

"A champion," his dad agreed. "And a great lady."

He scratched his head suddenly, sending his tall white chef's hat awry. "Help me hang this poster, Ol. It just came from the Department of Health. It shows how to perform the Heimlich maneuver."

"Oh, I know about that," Arthur said. "Beany Allen's uncle saved a rich lady's life when she was choking on a piece of steak. He squeezed under her rib cage like the Heimlich maneuver says, and that piece of steak just came right out. She wanted to give Beany's uncle a reward but he said no thanks, it was all in a day's work."

"What's Beany Allen's uncle do?" Oliver said.

"He's an auto mechanic," Arthur said.

"He's also a dope," Oliver said. "You wouldn't catch me turning down any reward from a rich lady."

"U. Crumm's rich," Arthur said. "You oughta see her car."

Just then, U. Crumm pulled up in her big white Caddy with its tail fins gleaming and its chrome trim ablaze.

"Heap big squaw," Oliver said.

"I *told* you she was a big shot," Arthur said.

"I've come to inspect the fireworks," U. Crumm said.

Oliver's mom and dad led U. Crumm to the boxes marked CAUTION: FLAMMABLE that were stacked against the wall.

"Very good, everything seems to be in order," U. Crumm said. "Is that gingerbread I smell?"

Oliver's mom and dad took U. Crumm into the kitchen so she could inspect the gingerbread, too.

That night, at dusk, Oliver and Arthur set their trap a second time.

"Tonight's a full moon," Oliver said. "That means good luck."

Later, that same moon woke Oliver up with a long, bright finger poked right in his eye. He sat up and put one foot down, on his way to calling Arthur to ask if he was asleep. Then he decided to go back to sleep instead.

In the early morning, with the dew still thick on the grass, they set out again.

"Braves tread softly, carry heap big stick," Oliver said.

"Teddy Roosevelt said that and he wasn't an Indian, he was president," Arthur replied.

"You're a know-it-all, Arthur," Oliver said. "Know that?"

They had almost reached the trap when Edna went wild. She barked like a wild thing and chased her tail round and round in circles.

"I told you, it's a cougar!" Arthur said.

"Smells like skunk to me," Oliver said.

As they crept closer Oliver said, "Don't scare him. Else he'll spray us."

It *was* a skunk, a very unfriendly skunk, that they had trapped.

Slowly, carefully, Oliver inched up to the trap and released the catch so the skunk could go free.

"Take off, bozo," Oliver told the skunk.

The skunk waddled halfway out of the trap, looking to the left, then the right.

Edna barked and bobbed and weaved, like a prizefighter looking for some action.

She got it.

Carefully, the skunk took aim and fired.

"Whoa!" Oliver ducked, too late. Heroes never got sprayed by skunks. Heroes never ducked either, he was sure.

Arthur clutched his chest as if he'd been shot.

Edna leaped high in the air and came down like a stone.

"That smell makes my eyes smart," Arthur said.

"Too bad it missed the rest of you," Oliver said. He felt shriveled and sad and unheroic.

Edna only whimpered.

"What'll we do, Ol?" Arthur said.

"Fake it," Oliver decided. "We just pretend nothing happened."

"You think anyone will buy that?"

"Probably not," Oliver said.

Edna lay on her back, all four feet sticking straight up in the air.

"You think she's dead, Ol?" Arthur said.

"Nah, she only wishes she were," Oliver said.

☆ 8 ☆
TOMATO-JUICE BATH

Oliver's mom smelled them coming. She met them at the door.

"Get out of those clothes and into the tub," she said. "All three of you. Yes, Edna, that means you too."

"Close your eyes," Oliver's dad said. "This is for your own good. Ours, too."

Oliver's mom and dad emptied four restaurant-size cans of tomato juice on the heads of Oliver, Arthur, and Edna.

"Sometimes this does the trick," Oliver's dad said.

"If it doesn't work this time," Oliver's mom said, "I don't know what we'll do."

"Lock 'em up in the woodshed until the Fourth of July party's over," Oliver's dad said.

"The show must go on," Oliver said.

"Why?" asked Arthur.

In the morning, they still smelled of skunk.

"*Wooeee*," said one of the men who was at the Blue Burd putting up the party tent. "You guys are pretty ripe. He got you good, huh?"

"Hey, boys," another man said, "you take

yourselves a bath in tomato juice. That'll fix you up. That's the ticket, tomato juice."

"We already did," Oliver said.

"I can hardly see," Arthur complained, squinting into the sun. "I got skunk *and* tomato juice in my eyes and my ears *and* up my nose. My mom said to get out of the house or she might go crazy."

"Better make yourselves scarce when the guests start arriving," Oliver's dad said. "Lay low and hope the wind's blowing in the right direction."

"Don't forget, Ol, keep an eye on U. Crumm," Arthur said. "This is your big chance to be a hero. The minute she starts choking—on account of she doesn't chew each bite fifteen times like you're supposed to—get in there and start squeezing. And we split the reward for saving her life fifty-fifty. This is it, Ol. Your big chance. Try not to blow it, like you did all the other times."

"All what other times?" Oliver said, on the defensive.

49

"Well . . ." Arthur began ticking off on his fingers. "When you went to rescue me from drowning and I could already touch bottom. Number one. Then the checkout girl saved your life, instead of you saving hers. Number two. Then instead of you getting Charlie down, the firemen had to go and get you. Number three.

"Plus," Arthur said, "we were gonna trap a muskrat or maybe a woodchuck, and look what we got. That's number four, Ol. That's a lot, four."

"So?" Oliver said.

"Get your act together, Ol, okay?" Arthur said.

Oliver and Arthur lurked in the bushes, watching the folks arrive.

Oliver brooded. It had all begun when U. Crumm slipped on the ice and smashed him flat. Nothing had gone right after that. He'd been going steadily downhill ever since.

U. Crumm owed him one, Oliver figured.

☆ 9 ☆
FIREWORKS

U. Crumm got first place in the chow line.
It was she who was to set off the fireworks,
and she needed nourishment in the worst
way.

Oliver got U. Crumm in his sight and
never let her out of it.

"I'll just have a tiny bit of everything,"
U. Crumm said. She'd brought her own
plate, which was about the size of a small
trampoline.

"I can't stand those tiny little plates they
give you," she said to no one in particular.

"I smell skunk," many people said, wrin-
kling their noses and peering around.

Oliver's eyes followed U. Crumm's fork and knife and spoon on the busy trip to and from her mouth. She ate piles of potato salad, gobs of gravy, heaps of ribs and fried chicken. Chocolate cake and strawberry shortcake with whipped cream. Hot dogs and hamburgers and macaroni salad.

U. Crumm gobbled everything in sight and went back for more.

But never once did her jaws stop moving, never once did she falter and choke, much less turn blue. She even swallowed what must have been bushels of olives, pits and all.

Oliver watched, dismayed.

U. Crumm chewed slowly, carefully, chewing every mouthful at least ten times. The food slid down nice and easy.

There was nothing to be done. There was no hope.

Then, at last, it was dark. Time for the fireworks.

Aware that every eye was upon her, though she wasn't counting Oliver's, U. Crumm wiped the last crumb from her mouth and rose to the occasion.

"Match, please," U. Crumm said in her carrying voice. A match was handed to her. She touched it to the rocket, the biggest, boldest rocket, which was to start the festivities. The night sky shattered into a thousand shards of red, white, and blue.

"*Oooooohhhh*," the crowd sighed. "See how beautiful. Look at that. Wonderful."

On and on it went. The sky was criss-crossed by all the colors of the rainbow. And a few more besides.

Finally, the boxes of fireworks were empty. The last Roman candle had fizzled, the last flare had fallen to earth.

"First-rate job!" Oliver's dad cried, pumping U. Crumm's hand in thanks. "Perhaps you'd care for a little refreshment before you leave?"

"Oh, definitely," U. Crumm said. "Setting off fireworks always makes me hungry."

U. Crumm would surely choke now, Oliver thought. This was it. This was what he'd waited for.

Down the hatch went pretzels, one last piece of pepperoni pizza, a handful of Cheeseroonies, a few tacos for luck.

U. Crumm then climbed aboard her big

white Caddy with the gleaming tail fins and the shining chrome trim and headed for home.

Oliver and Arthur crept out of the bushes.

"What did we do wrong?" Arthur said, close to tears.

"I wanted to be rich and famous," Oliver said sadly. "But most of all, I wanted to be a hero. I blew it. I can't do anything right."

Briefly, he thought of Carrot Hill Nursery School, of Ms. Mabel saying "Oud" and pointing to the door. Of his mother saying, "Poor little Oliver. What's to become of him?"

I'm a loser, Oliver thought. Losers are never heroes.

He felt very sad, very sorry for himself.

☆ 10 ☆
HEAP BIG
HERO!

"Good night! Thanks a million. It was grand!" the guests called, leaving the party with reluctant feet.

A few stragglers still hung around, enjoying the soft night air, turning their faces to the stars, hoping for a last look at an unexpected rocket going off up there.

Edna, meanwhile, crept under the tables, cleaning up all the delicious tidbits that had fallen.

She had forgotten she didn't like leftovers. She pigged out. It was Independence Day, after all, and that called for a feast.

And feast Edna did.

When she spied a half-eaten chicken leg, Edna snapped it up and scarfed it down before anyone else could get it. Fried chicken was her favorite.

The bone stuck halfway down. Edna turned blue without ado, although it was hard to tell under all that orange hair.

Edna choked noisily and her big brown eyes rolled back in her head.

"Quick, somebody! Edna's choking!" Oliver's mom cried. "Somebody do something, quick!"

Oliver's time had come.

He grabbed hold of Edna below her rib cage and gave several short, sharp squeezes, the way he'd learned at school, as well as from the Heimlich maneuver poster at the Blue Burd. The chicken bone popped out of Edna like a cork out of a bottle.

Edna gave a mighty sigh and licked Oliver's cheek as if it were a chocolate ice cream cone.

"No two ways about it, Ol," said Oliver's

dad, patting him on the back. "You saved Edna's life."

"You deserve a medal, Oliver," his mom said, hugging him.

"Odds on Oliver!" shouted the last remaining guests.

"Heap big hero," said Arthur. "How."

"Well, it wasn't easy," Oliver said.

That night, excitement and happiness racketed around inside Oliver, keeping him awake. Edna couldn't sleep either. Back and forth she paced, toenails clicking noisily on the floor.

"Cut it out, Edna," Oliver said sleepily. "Don't forget, if it wasn't for me, you'd be only a memory right this minute."

In answer, Edna leaped up onto the bed and snuggled down cozily on Oliver's pillow. She barked once or twice to let him know how she felt.

"You're welcome," Oliver said. He fell asleep then, a big smile on his face. It was the smile of a hero. At long last.